Domina by Accident

~o~

Domina Diaries

Book 1

Nicole

TIMEA TOKES

DEDICATION

To all my lovely readers out there. Remember, no matter what your dreams are (naughty or not), you have everything you need to make them come true.

If you love my writing style, please check out my other titles on Amazon, and follow me on my blog & website for a FREE pdf copy of Squirm Under My Watch, FREE Audiobooks, and other goodies, to say a personal thank you to you all.

I am also hosting a monthly signed paperback giveaway, with at least 2 winners each month. So, please stay tuned, and share the love that's deep inside all of you.

Thank you!

www.timeatokes.com

ACKNOWLEDGMENTS

All characters and events in these stories are purely fictional, therefore any resemblance to real people (living or dead) or events is a coincidence.

All characters would be at least 18 years of age, too, should they be real.

Caution: Contains descriptive sex scenes and adult contents.

Intended for a mature audience of at least 18+ (or more, depending on your country of residence and the local law).

Chapter 1

I take a sip of my violet gin, noting gladly that it contains more gin than lemonade. I sure as hell need something strong to get me through the night. I even wonder how long it is before I can ask for the bill and sneak out gracefully, keeping the little dignity I still have.

I reckon that five minutes after I arrived isn't the right answer to that question. Maybe half an hour? A couple laughs in the next booth and I look down at the menu in sheer embarrassment. I am a bit angry at Amanda, too, although this is hardly her fault. She couldn't have known that the first guy I was supposed to meet through the app would be a no-show.

I close my eyes, reminding myself that I need to chill. Being forty-five, a recently divorced woman, and now officially a single mum isn't the best conversation starter anyway, so I guess I should be glad that he never turned up. A blush creeps up my neck when I recall our conversation from the night before, and all the other options I had. Namely, none.

Joshua was the only man interested in dating me, even despite everything I am. Well, what exactly am I? With all these labels society put on me, I kind of forgot that I used to be a woman, and a sexy one, too. I could have anyone I wanted in my early days. Too bad that my husband (pardon, ex-husband) didn't appreciate that fact.

Fine, he might have done the opposite and appreciated it too much. He wanted me to become a hotwife as they call it nowadays. In my early days, we had a different name for the kind of woman he wanted me to become. Well, he wanted me to explore my options while still being with him, and I decided that wasn't an option for me.

And now, I'm ready to do the exact same thing. A sigh escapes me when someone plops down in the seat opposite me, disturbing my wayward thoughts. I am about to tell them to go away when I gasp, realising that it's Joshua. He was just late, not a no-show. My heart does a double flip, and not only because he didn't let me down in the end.

'Hey, how is it going? Sorry for being late.'

He says in a voice as smooth as the gin I'm sipping, yet with just the same amount of delicious bite, too. I gulp, taking another sip.

'Don't mention it, it's fine.'

I reply, trying to sound cool, or whatever they call it nowadays. He shakes his head, providing a bunch of red roses from behind his back. My heart skips a beat when he takes my hand, places a kiss onto the back of it, before handing me the flowers.

'No, it's not okay. A beautiful woman like you should never have to wait.'

My blush deepens, and I have no idea what to say. I guess looking him up and down wouldn't hurt, as he is doing the same to me right now, and he doesn't even feel ashamed of it. So many things changed since I went on a date last time that I feel like I have to learn everything all over again.

Joshua smiles at me, probably encouraging me to take a closer look. My mouth goes dry when I take him in, from the dark caramel coloured hair that's cut short on the sides and held together by gel on top, to the chiselled chin and cute dimples on both sides of his lips. And those lips... They are so luscious and full, and kissable. His muscles strain against his white T-shirt that says *'I'm the Boss'*, and I believe him. Even though he is only twenty-three, his body screams authority and experience. Lots of it, too.

I gulp again, downing my drink. I have no idea why he agreed to meet me, and it might even be a sick joke for all I know. What would a man like him do with a woman like me? I'm almost twice his age, and even if we did date, he would end up swapping me for an eighteen-year-old within a month. There aren't many guarantees in life, but that's definitely one of them.

I shake my head sadly, while Joshua's green eyes take me in. I notice the golden speckles in them, and I'm about to count them, before I stop myself. No, this has already gone too far in my head, and we haven't even spoken to each other yet. Not properly anyway. I'm so out of my league here that I can only hope nobody notices us and I can make an excuse. Of course, I'm out of luck.

'What can I get you and your...'

The waiter looks at us, embarrassed, glancing at the bouquet of red roses Joshua just handed to me. My hands only shake a tiny bit. Joshua looks at the waiter confidently, taking my hand in his at the same time. I think I stop breathing.

'My fiancée and I would like to get the bill, please. Considering the quality of the service, we will take our anniversary date somewhere else.'

It's the waiter's turn to blush, and he mumbles something under his breath that I don't catch. Not that I'm paying too much attention, either. Joshua shoots me an apologetic smile, shrugging and pulling his hand back once the waiter is gone.

'Sorry about that. Some people just don't get us.'

He says it in such a sweet and innocent way, as if this was the most natural thing on Earth. I let out a sigh, not wanting to remind him that I could be his mother. Besides, I am definitely not having motherly thoughts about him, let's just say that. But am I even allowed to do this? I mean, at the age of forty-five I should be more sensible, right?

Amanda's voice echoes in my mind, and she is right I'm sure. I need to enjoy my time, because I'm not getting any younger. According to her, I wasted my prime years on a useless husband anyway, so I might as well start fresh. I force myself to smile and reach out to caress Joshua's hand, knowing too well that there is some truth behind her words.

'It's alright, I'm not hungry anyway. What do you say we get out of here?'

I bite my lower lip, unable to believe I just said that. And yet, I had everything planned out from the beginning. We discussed it. Joshua confessed that he wasn't looking for a long-term relationship this time, and neither was I. According to Amanda, even if it doesn't work out, I can cross this off my bucket list and say that I shagged a guy almost half my age. Joshua's eyes light up and he winks at me, leaving a twenty on the table.

'Sure thing, gorgeous. Show me the way.'

With a girlish giggle, I take the offered hand and we run out of the restaurant, followed by a few awkward glances and raised eyebrows. I even leave the roses behind, something I would normally feel guilty about. But the funny thing about it is that I don't care anymore. Twenty years of being unhappily married does that to you...

Chapter 2

~o~

I can't believe this is happening. Joshua is waiting for me in the bedroom, and I'm here, having a slight panic attack. Fair enough, I never thought I would end up having sex with anyone else apart from my husband. It's been so long that I almost forgot how to do this. I mean, I prepared the room, and we talked about some kinky stuff beforehand, to make it easier, but still.

To think that I could do this without hesitating, that was a mistake. My heart is threatening to jump out of my chest, and my palms are sweaty. I keep looking at the outfit Joshua picked for me, the now familiar blush creeping up my neck. I'm pretty sure even my boobs are crimson right now.

Amanda was right after all. Dating after forty doesn't have to be difficult, it's just a bit different. Instead of dinner dates, you end up wearing latex, covering up all your flaws, and jumping into bed with the guy (or girl, because, nowadays, everything and anything goes).

Part of me wonders why I could never do this for Dave, but I guess some things you are meant to improve after you leave your spouse. You don't want to change for their sake, only to do the exact thing you didn't want to do, for yourself this time. Too bad that for me, it's my sex life that needed to be put on hold till then.

'Is everything alright in there?'

Joshua asks through the closed doors, and I sigh, pushing my boobs up higher in the black corset. I must admit, the sexy lingerie he picked for me fits perfectly and accentuates my assets. Not that I have many of those, mind you, but I have always been proud of my boobs (especially since I was pregnant with Ashley).

'Yes, all good. I will be out in a second.'

I re-apply my makeup (not that I know how to do it, but at least I can pretend), then use the perfume Dave bought me for our last anniversary. I must admit, this makes me feel extremely naughty, especially considering that he would have wanted me to wear it on my adventures anyway. I run my hands through my blond curls, taking one more look in the mirror, before heading out to the bedroom.

'God, you are so beautiful.'

Joshua says and I stop dead in my tracks, looking around in a mixture of shock and amusement. The bed is littered with toys (and not the kiddy-type, either), and Joshua has somehow ended up tying himself to the bedpost. There is something red in his left palm, and after looking at it more carefully, I note reluctantly that it's a ball-gag. I clear my throat, ignoring his comment on my own attire, considering that I can hardly comment on his non-existent one.

'Look, Joshua, I appreciate the effort, but I'm not into being dominated. I never let my ex-husband do it, and I certainly won't let a...'

Joshua raises an eyebrow.

'Well, if you haven't noticed, I am the one tied up here, not you.'

He has a point, so I motion for him to carry on, while I walk around in my ridiculously high heels, assessing the situation.

'Nicole, I know you just came out of a messy divorce, and I also know that dating isn't easy for you.'

Well, that's an understatement, I want to say, but I resist, knowing that he is only trying to be nice. As I don't say a word, he carries on:

'But if you ask me, women like you deserve to be worshipped. And I would love to give you anything and everything you need.'

I raise an eyebrow, looking at his toned, very naked figure and his obvious attraction to me.

'Anything?'

He nods, gulping. I notice that the gold speckles in his green eyes grow larger, making his eyes seem as big as saucers and as shiny as stars.

'Anything. All you need to do is ask.'

I purse my lips, feeling bold all of a sudden. Running a hand up his thigh, I watch as his cock twitches in sheer anticipation. It's been a long time since I had this sort of effect on someone, and having him do anything I want is certainly something new. But isn't that what Dave wanted me to do? If I'm honest with myself, it wasn't the fact that he asked me to do all that, but rather the way he did it. He didn't give me a choice, and I believe that defeats the object.

'Well, I'm not sure what to ask, if I'm honest.'

I admit sheepishly, and Joshua nods, understanding. Of course, I have many things I would love him to do to me, but I surely can't ask for those, can I? Dave never wanted to do them, so...

'I get it. I will be your first, and that's such an honour that not many can experience. So, thank you.'

I hum to myself, not sure what to say to that. I thought that the crotchless panties or the latex gloves would do the trick and make me wonderwoman, but unfortunately that's not how this works. Joshua smiles at me gently, lowering his voice to a whisper.

'Let me guide you this time then, so when you meet your next date, you will know what to do.'

I want to ask him whether all the guys his age are this way, but I don't want to offend him. Besides, I guess there is nothing wrong with wanting to be dominated. Since *Fifty Shades of Grey*, every woman wants it, so why do we judge men who do, too?

'Okay, so, what do I ask?'

His smile widens, and an excited sparkle lights up his beautiful irises.

'Well, first, you ask me to lick your boots. And before you say anything, that's a must. Partly because I will enjoy worshipping you that way, and partly because it will make you feel powerful. Ready?'

No.

'Fine.'

He nods, then purses his lips.

'One more thing before we begin.'

I raise an eyebrow and he continues:

'You need to act like you owned me. Think about it as roleplaying. You are the boss, you decide what happens and when. Really, Nicole, you don't even know the power you have over me – the power you could have over any guy, and not just my age, either.'

I nod, not entirely believing him, but willing to give this a go.

Oh, the kind of things you do to get laid in the modern day and age...

~o~

Chapter 3

~o~

walk up to the bed, then push the heel of my black lace-up boots in Joshua's nose. Literally.

'I'm so sorry, are you okay?'

I gasp, but he smirks at me, wagging his manicured eyebrows. My insecurities kick in once again when I realise that he probably spends more time in front of the mirror than I do.

'I'm more than fine. I can worship such a goddess as yourself, so how couldn't I be?'

I want to roll my eyes at him, or tell him that he is being silly. I'm not beautiful, and I am certainly not a woman to be worshipped. Hell, my marriage is a prime example. I let Dave treat me the way he did, and it was as much my fault as it was his. But the way Joshua looks at me now, his golden-green eyes sparkling in the dim light, challenging me to take control, is intoxicating. I do feel like a completely different woman. I feel wanted. Desired. In control of my life again.

'Come on, Nicole, you can do this. I need you to do this for us. Please?'

I let out a sigh, reaching for the riding crop Joshua placed on the bedside cabinet earlier. It feels alien in my hand, the smoothness of the silk on top, contrasted by the roughness of the leather at the bottom, and yet I feel like the riding crop has been my lifelong companion. Strange that we get so attached to things so quickly, but never to people.

I run my fingers along the stiff rod, thrilled by the mixed sensations the different materials evoke within me, and Joshua lets out a whimpering sound. It is a guttural, almost animalistic sound, one I never heard from Dave. But then again, our love life was dull at best. I still remember the times I sneaked to the bathroom to finish his job.

'Nicole, please...'

Joshua begs, and although I'm not entirely sure what he is begging me for, I feel more in tune with my role. I should look at it as acting, he said. *Fine*. I clear my throat, pressing my heel into his muscular chest.

'It's not Nicole anymore.'

My voice betrays me, being loud and authoritative, and Joshua's eyes glaze over instantly. I even swat my palm with the riding crop, wincing slightly at the stingy burn. I must admit though that the pain does wonders to the flow of my juices, despite everything.

'Yes, Mistress. Although I'm not worthy of your mercy, but can you forgive me for being so inconsiderate?'

Okay, I want to tell him to tune it down a notch, because this is too much, but his eyes convince me otherwise. I want to try something out, so I touch the leather on the underside of the crop, then gently tap it against my palm, gauging his reaction. It doesn't hurt this time, and an unfamiliar sensation rushes through me. Shame filled with arousal, but there is more. There is the hint of unlimited power, and it's intoxicating.

I don't have to wait long, because Joshua's cock tells me exactly how much he likes what he sees. My stomach fills with flutters, and watching his erect cock jerk (which is around the same length as the riding crop) is a heady sensation. I clear my throat again, pushing my heel slightly into his chest, hopefully not causing too much pain.

'Well, inconsiderate men need to be punished, don't you think?'

I muse, still caressing the crop, while keeping an eye on his cock. Joshua gulps, pulling on his restraints. He even drops the ball gag. I wonder whether I am supposed to pick it up and silence him with it, but I guess that would defeat the object, so I try to forget about it for now. Not that it's easy, the red ball screaming out to me from halfway under the bed.

'Yes, please, Mistress. I will do anything you ask.'

I nod, guessing that's the codework for the roleplay we agreed on earlier. A funny thought crosses my mind: I'm almost reciting a script, and yet, I'm more wet than I have ever been. But right now, I don't have the time or the energy to figure out how I feel. Right now, I need to dominate Joshua and finally get laid the way I was supposed to for all these years.

Closing my eyes, I let all the built-up tension of my failed marriage go. Ashley will grow up to be a powerful woman, and I will make sure she doesn't marry someone like her father. Whether Dave sticks around or not, she will make it just fine. And as for me, well... I open my eyes again, looking deep into Joshua's green pair.

'I think you are right.'

I clear my throat, shaking my head. Joshua smiles at me, and I decide to start again, pointing the crop at his muscular chest. He inhales sharply and I move the crop to his erect nipple, circling it with leisurely movements. Maybe I could do this, so I convince myself to start again. Just how many clean slates does a woman get in a situation like this? It seems like the answer is as many as needed, because Joshua looks up at me with beady eyes.

'I mean, you are right when you say you don't deserve my mercy. But I will be merciful regardless. I will allow you to lick my boots, because that's all you are good for, anyway.'

I want to ask him whether I did alright or not, but I don't have to, because he starts on his given task straight away. I am shocked and paralysed, watching this twenty-three-year-old man dart his tongue out and lick my boots with so much passion that it makes me blush. I can't help but imagine him licking me out somewhere more intimate that way, and I guess that's the point.

I fake a moan and I watch his cock jerk again. The next moan I don't have to fake, because his tongue snakes between the laces, tickling the top of my foot. There is something so erotic in being in control, it's unbelievable. And it's not just that. The way Joshua looks at me, like I was the best thing that ever happened to him, and he doesn't even know me.

Maybe that's why…

A nasty thought tries to push its way to the surface, but one more longing look from Joshua shoos it away. I blush a little more as I pick up the courage and whisper:

'Now I want you to lick my pussy.'

Joshua licks his lips seductively.

'With pleasure. Just sit on my face and show me how you want it.'

He says breathlessly, and even my breath catches in my throat as I move my leg to the other side of his face, grabbing onto the headboard to keep my balance while I position myself above his lips. My whole body is shaking with a mixture of frustration, humiliation and arousal at the promise of what he is about to do. But of course, nothing is that simple in my life. Just as I'm about to shove my pussy in Joshua's face (something that would have been unimaginable a day ago), my phone rings in my purse and I facepalm myself.

'Amanda…'

I whisper, and Joshua frowns.

'You forgot my name already?'

I let out a frustrated laugh.

'No, it's not that. My friend is calling, and I should probably pick up.'

Joshua looks at me for a long moment, and I can't help finding our predicament a tad bit funny. Him tied up underneath me, me halfway in his face with one leg perched above his shoulder, the other one still on the ground. I know they say that at my age, one of my legs is always on the other side, but I'm pretty sure that's not what they mean. My phone keeps ringing in the background, and I know this is the moment that could make it or break it for me. And then it does exactly both.

~o~

Chapter 4

~o~

After a long moment, Joshua closes his eyes, nodding.

'Ah, I get it. She is calling you to get you out of your awful date, because you never gave her the sign that everything went well.'

My blush deepens, and I wonder whether I should be having this conversation while I'm so exposed. Joshua's eyes dart down to my naked pussy lips underneath the latex outfit, and my mouth goes dry.

'I'm sorry, Joshua, I forgot. It isn't like this happens to me every day, you know.'

He shrugs (well, as much as his restraints allow it).

'I don't see why. You have everything any man could ever want.'

I blush some more, shifting in my increasingly uncomfortable position. Let's face it: Kama Sutra only works while you have the muscles to support you in the crazy positions.

'You are kind and a nice man. But I still can't see why you would want this.'

I motion to the restraints and he lets out a sigh.

'Look. To the outside world, I am always in charge. I have to be. But in my private life, it's nice to let go once in a while. And for women, it's the opposite. Society never lets them be in control, so this is their perfect opportunity to shine. And when I say shine, I mean...'

He licks his lips again, glancing at my pussy and the juices that are now dripping onto his chest. My blush deepens, probably making me look like a lobster now, and my cheeks burn from the shame, but weirdly enough, that's all that happens. I don't jump away, nor do I run for the door. Suddenly he looks up, his eyes glazed over again.

'Nicole, I understand if this isn't your scene, and I get that you probably don't want to do this. But don't you at least want to try what it would feel like before you reject it completely? You might even enjoy it, you know.'

For a moment, an old story comes to mind. I still remember when Ashley was born and I was craving sushi. I never tried it in my entire life, so I made up all these excuses to avoid the temptation. Because new things could end really badly. But then, when I left Dave and had a bold moment, I bought some and after letting it sit in my fridge for three days, I eventually convinced myself that I needed to eat it, otherwise I might as well have thrown that money out the window.

And the bottom line is that the first bite was epic. The whole experience made me regret that I bailed out on doing it so many times, because I felt like I wasted that time, while I could have enjoyed more of the good stuff. If I'm honest, I don't even know when I became so scared of trying new things.

I glance towards my bag that's sitting on the counter. I could call Amanda up and get out of here, or I could stay and give it a go. Either way, nobody is going to judge me. I just have to make sure I don't judge myself. I'm not saying that my experience with Joshua will be the same as with the sushi, but it doesn't have to be, either. I need to realise and accept that new experiences still shape my life. Yes, even after forty-five. Both the good *and* the bad.

I turn my attention back to the man in front of me, focusing on the way the heat from his body radiates into mine, as if we were already one. I try to clear my thoughts and get rid of all my expectations. I mean, what's the worst thing that could happen? Me having to go to the bathroom to finish off what he started? I did that with Dave, so it wouldn't be anything new. And if that happens, I will just chuck this experience behind closed doors in my mind, never to be touched again.

'So, are you going to lick me out or not?'

I ask, hoping that my voice is challenging and husky, but I probably only sound annoyed and bitchy. What I say does the trick though, as Joshua leans in for better access. I grab the headboard again, making it easier for him. The moment his tongue darts out and licks at my clit tentatively, time slows, and I am temporarily transported back to the moment I first tasted that sushi.

I even forget my plan to bring the riding crop down on his nipple. That probably would have hurt plenty anyway. Instead I close my eyes, tilt my head back and let the crop fall from my hands as I relish in the sensations Joshua's tongue is giving me. He is lapping at my clit too slowly though, even after it's swollen enough for him to increase the pace.

My insecurities surface again, purely because Dave never listened whenever I told him he wasn't doing it right. He claimed that I would get to enjoy his ways eventually. And when that never happened, somehow it ended up being my fault. I grip the headboard tighter as Joshua's tongue pushes into my hole. I know I need to speak up now, or be silent for ever (well, at least till the night is over). My way never worked, so I decide to try Amanda's and say what's on my mind:

'Joshua, only lick my clit, and do it faster and harder than before.'

I try not to sound too authoritative, but his guttural moan reminds me that it's exactly what's expected of me. And my, I'm not disappointed. A tear rolls down my cheek when he obeys, withdrawing his tongue from my pussy and picking up where he left off, taking my swollen clit between his luxurious lips.

'Yes, just like that.'

I breathe, getting lost in the sensations. Sparks fly behind my closed eyelids, and I know I'm getting near to an orgasm. His tongue moves expertly over my clit, licking up and down, then sucking the nub in, nibbling at it like it was cotton candy. The vibrations from his moans shake me to my core, and I can feel my whole body shudder. Suddenly I'm so desperate to have him inside me that I can't take his torture anymore. Lifting my leg up and over his head, I quickly get off the bed – or try to anyway, landing on my bum instead.

~o~

Chapter 5

~o~

Air leaves my lungs with a silent huff as I land on the floor, very unladylike. Thankfully, the shock and the shame is worse than the pain. I stumble to my feet noisily, heat rising in my entire body.

'Shit, are you okay?'

Joshua asks, genuine concern in his eyes and voice. I check myself for injuries (fuck it, he knows my age, so I might as well act like it), and after stating that I don't have any broken bones, just a bruised ego, I nod, forcing a smile. I even remember the ball gag, picking it up from underneath the bed.

'I'm fine. But I must say, your skills are highly questionable.'

He raises an eyebrow, then, when I reach behind his head and pick up the riding crop, too, the golden pecks in his eyes reflect understanding.

'I'm sorry, Mistress. It won't happen again.'

I nod, my heart thumping so hard and fast I am tempted to call an ambulance, just in case I have a heart attack and Joshua ends up the same way the poor woman did in the movie *Gerard's Game*. It takes me considerable effort not to reach for the phone and to push my anxiety aside. However, staying in character is becoming surprisingly easier.

'Of course it won't. You know why?'

I ask, hitting the riding crop against my palm. This time, I both expect and want the sting that follows. He shakes his head, glancing at my hands.

'Because I'm taking charge of my own pleasure this time.'

I look at his lean body, and his still erect cock, finally realising that I can truly do anything I want with him. Funny how my fantasy falls short in this situation, because all I can think of is riding his cock.

Not sure that would be enough for him though, I need to improvise, and as such, I decide to use the props he provided me with. I reach up and place the red ball gag in his mouth, then regret the decision straight away, knowing that I would need reassurance, which is something he can't give anymore. He nods though, which I guess will have to do.

Excitement pooling at the bottom of my belly, I try to climb onto the bed in an erotic way, although the ridiculously high heels aren't really making my job easy. Instead of doing a stunt I couldn't even perform at the age of twenty, I take the riding crop between my teeth, then move to the edge of the bed and crawl my way up from where Joshua's feet are. Judging by the way his eyes bulge, watching my boobs rise and fall, I made the right call. Now all I need to do is sit on his cock and rock us both into ecstasy.

Of course, my phone (or rather Amanda) choses this moment to vibrate in my bag for the second time. But this time is different. I shut the noise out of my mind, and focus solely on the man underneath me. Reaching down, I run my fingers along his shaft, already moaning at his length. Don't even get me started on the fact that I can hardly wrap my fingers around his girth.

I clear my throat, positioning his cock at my entrance, while balancing my heels on either side of him. This wouldn't work, because I'm too high up in the air and there is no way I could ride him without breaking a leg or two (either his or mine). I roll my eyes, silently cursing at the boots, then lower myself down on my knees, my pussy finally being level with his cock. The tip pushes in on its own accord, and a puff of air escapes my lungs once again.

Deciding to keep the riding crop secure between my lips, I push down, so his cock can be secure between my *other* lips. Then I simply rock my hips until his shaft completely disappears. My eyes roll to the back of my head, and I'm seeing all kinds of crazy stuff. I never took drugs in my life, but I assume this is how it would feel like: in control, yet losing your grip on reality.

Joshua rolls his hips, his cock pushing higher up and touching a sweet spot inside that Dave could never find. I moan loudly, grinding my hips to match his movements. It's no longer about who's in control. It's about pure pleasure, and suddenly everything I knew about sex before Dave comes back to me. My hips move in ways I almost forgot, and my inner muscles clench around Joshua's cock as and when I want them to.

I'm not only in control of my own orgasm or his, but I am in control of my own body, and that's not something I felt since I got pregnant. Feeling like I need to prove a point, I take the riding crop out from between my lips and bring it down on Joshua's chest. His cock jerks inside me, almost sending me over the edge instantly, but I hold back and so does he.

All I can hear is the rush of blood in my veins, and our panting mixing in the darkness of the hotel room. I wonder what Amanda would say if I did take her call. I wonder what Dave would say, if I did decide to take him up on his offer and become a hotwife.

But there is no point in getting lost in the what ifs. That was always my issue. I simply couldn't live in the here and now. So, to keep me in reality, I bring the riding crop down on Joshua's balls, punishing him as much as I'm punishing myself. They tighten straight away, and his cock swells, threatening to burst. I reach down to caress them, accidentally finding a position that will send me into a frenzy I'm sure.

Joshua seems to know, too, and he might be fed up of me being in charge after all, because he shifts his hips, pushing the tip of his cock right against that sweet spot, rubbing it with such a force that a thousand stars explode behind my eyelids and I see more crazy stuff. Unicorns, mermaids, you name it. Joshua's cock makes me believe in magic again and is definitely better than drugs.

He keeps rubbing the tip of his cock against my G-spot until I have a second, and then a third orgasm, and he finally releases his load too, stretching my inner walls in an almost painful way. I can still feel his cock spurt and twitch, and it takes my muscles a while to relax their hold on his shaft, too. I guess the unicorns and mermaids are here to stay, and so is the feeling of power.

We rest like this for a while. Me in a weird, twisted position, grabbing his balls for support, still holding the riding crop. And him, well… Ball gag in mouth, spread out on the bed. I make a note to ask him later how he did it. Unless he is a descendant of Houdini, I doubt he could have tied himself up without help. And then it hits me. I use all my strength to sit up, his cock still buried deep inside my pussy.

'You aren't really tied up, are you? I mean, you could have got out anytime.'

Joshua closes his eyes for a moment before nodding, sliding his hand out from the loop. He removes the ball gag, licking his lips. I blush, remembering where those lips were earlier.

'You are right and I'm sorry. I guess I can't give up all my power, you know.'

I nod, understanding. I think I do know. Joshua clears his throat and I blush again, climbing down from his lap. Our bodies disengage with a loud pop, making me feel embarrassed and ashamed once again. Did I do the right thing?

'Um… I will call you?'

I say, but it sounds like a question. I'm not exactly sure whether it's his duty to say that or mine, considering that I was dominating him. Maybe all roles are reversed. He shakes his head, tilting his head to the side.

'No, you won't. But that's okay, Nicole. Just do one more thing for me, okay?'

I raise an eyebrow, partly at his candidness, and partly at the unspoken request.

'What's that?'

He smirks at me before looking me up and down, from the black too-high-heels to the crotchless panties and the latex corset. One of my gloves has fallen off somewhere, probably to be found by a shocked cleaner in the morning.

'Just never change. Trust me on this, because I would know. You make an excellent dominatrix.'

I'm not sure about that, but I nod anyway. Feeling bold and intoxicated by the way he still looks at me, I reach for my clothes and put them in my bag. Then, still feeling Joshua's eyes on me, I slip into my coat, wearing nothing else underneath, but the crotchless panties and the corset. I glance back over my shoulder, and he send me off with a reassuring nod.

Once outside, the crisp autumn air gets under my coat, caressing my bare pussy. I am fully aware that I'm dripping with Joshua's cum, and I'm also pretty sure that he is jerking off back in the hotel room right now. Part of me wants to go back and enjoy another round of pure pleasure, but there is another, more dominant part of me that knows that this was just the beginning of my journey.

A passer-by waves at me and I smile at him, wondering what he gets up to in the dead of the night. Everyone has a secret, and I think this might just be mine. My phone beeps again, and a smug smile appears on my lips when I realise that for once, I will be the one to shock Amanda with my story. She might not even believe me, but it doesn't matter. Something changed tonight and I got my life back. I got the old me back.

'I've missed you so much.'

I whisper in the dimming light, reaching for the strap on my coat to pull it tighter. Someone catcalls from the other side of the street, and my hand stops mid-air, my smile widening. I let my coat fall a little off my shoulders, and, just like a movie star, I walk off into the sunset, head held high, heels clicking on the pavement.

~o~

A tempting taste of other, bite-size erotica, from the naughty pen of Timea Tokes:

~o~

A SPECIAL CUP OF COFFEE
(SAMPLE)

Don't worry, this is a first for me, too..."
Ah, is that supposed to comfort me?
Very promising.

I try to pull on the restraints, but he has tied me up tightly. My heart is pounding, and I can't see a thing because of the blindfold. All I can do is wait helplessly until he figures out his next move, wondering how could I have gotten myself into this mess.

A mere hour ago I was sitting at the bar, minding my own business, drinking heavily, as if there was no tomorrow. Right up to the moment when the bartender offered to make me a special cup of coffee. Which I'm still waiting for, by the way.

Just saying.

Okay, I wasn't that naïve to think that we would actually be drinking coffee, cuddling on his couch, no. And as I said, I didn't want that anyway. I wanted hot, steamy, and kinky sex. And although he hasn't touched me yet, not in that way anyway, this whole situation is kinky alright.

"Just try to relax and clear your mind..."

He is really getting into this. Does he have a guidebook that he is citing from? I must admit that hearing his voice alone makes me shiver all over. It is sexy as hell, and I can already feel the previous dampness of my thong worsening by the minute. I wonder how long is he going to keep me suspended like this? It's funny how you lose all of your senses when you can't see.

No kidding!

Although I can hear his voice, but only when he allows me to, and I still can't tell where it's coming from. For all I know he could be standing in the doorway, ready to lock me in, leaving me to suffer for God knows how long. I sure as hell hope he isn't planning to make that special cup of coffee *right now.*

But judging by what he just said, I guess I need to do the opposite. In fact, my mind is the only thing that's working perfectly well right now. And my survival instincts, of course. I begin to regret that I didn't listen to my friends. I should have waited for this kind of kink until I knew the guy, let alone trusted him.

Oh my God, I don't even know his name!

"You might feel a little bit cold. Try not to wiggle too much, okay?"

Okay, I was wrong. All my nerves are on edge, and I want to scream from the ice-cold sensation that's burning my left nipple right now.

Little bit cold?

Whatever he put on me makes me want to swear and scream, except I can't. All I can give out is a tiny whimper through my gritted teeth. I want to tell him to stop, to let me go, feeling embarrassed and exposed all of a sudden.

But as quickly as the thought forms in the back of my mind, it evaporates just as quickly when he takes my erect nipple into his mouth. His hot, wet tongue is a relief from the ice-cold sensation, and yet it feels a tad bit more painful, maybe because I am more sensitive than I ever was. He bites down gently, and I can feel the coldness on my right nipple, while he is stroking my left one with his tongue.

I gasp, getting lost in the mixed sensations of hot and cold, pain and pleasure. But it doesn't last long, and as much as I wanted him to stop at first, now I wish that he would continue the sweet torture. An involuntary moan leaves my lips, and he lets out a small chuckle.

"Don't worry, I have only just started."

His words send a jolt of electricity right down to my lady parts, and I'm sure I blush a little, too. I think about my black strapless dress, the black lace push-up bra and the black high heels scattered around the room. I'm not even sure he is wearing anything right now, as after a few passionate kisses, he moved straight onto the subject. He promised it to be fun, erotic and orgasmic.

The last part convinced me, and I'm more and more sure that he is a man who keeps his promises...

~o~

Kiss
&
Tell
Tail
Reverse Harem
Fairy Tales
1
Timea Tokes

Three
Policemen
&
Me
Reverse Harem
Chronicles
3
Timea Tokes

Other Books by Timea Tokes:

Paranormal Romance:
Her First Secret
Her Secret Admirer
His Secret Love
Their Last Secret
Her First And Last Secret Admirer

Erotic Short Stories:

Reverse Harem Chronicles:
Three Firemen & Me
Three Firemen & Me 2
Three Policemen & Me
Three Policemen & Me 2
Three Billionaires & Me

Reverse Harem Fairy Tales:
Kiss & Tell Tail

BDSM:
A Special Cup of Coffee – Pain and Pleasure

Hotwife:
Stuck & Shared

Holiday Erotica:
Mistletoe Boss
Dating The Author (Why Choose)
My Hitch-Hiking Valentine
The Bucket List
The Bucket List 2 - Damsel in Distress
Truth or Dare?

Exhibitionist & Voyeur:

Squirm Under My Watch
How About the Rooftop?
Don't Make A Sound

<u>Paranormal Erotica:</u>
Conjured Lover

<u>The Plumber Series:</u>
Seducing the Plumber 1: Sweet Time Waiting
Seducing the Plumber 2: Sweet Torture

<u>The Escort Series:</u>
The Escort's Taxi Ride
The Escort's Taxi Ride 2
The Escort's Taxi Ride 3

<u>The Good Neighbor Series (Bisexual, Why Choose):</u>
The Good Neighbor – An Unexpected Threesome
The Good Neighbor – Tied up by the Knight
The Good Neighbor – In the Backseat
The Good Neighbor – The Massage
The Good Neighbor – Guilty Pleasures

<u>Sweet yet Naughty:</u>
Forgotten
Blue Highlights

<u>Gay:</u>
The Stranger

<u>Collections of Short Stories:</u>
You Had Me At Kinky
You Had Me At Steamy
You Had Me At Rough

Coming Soon:

The Plumber's Excuse (2020)
Three Billionaires & Me 3 (2020)
Kiss & Tell Tail 4 (2020)
A Cupid Mistake (2021)
Hell's Bride (2021)
Domina by Choice (2020)

Follow Timea Tokes on:

Amazon @timea_tokes

Twitter @timea_tokes

Facebook @herfirstsecret

Goodreads @timea_tokes

Sign up to her newsletter, and have a look at her blog for more bite-size erotica, paranormal romance, reviews and more:

www.timeatokes.com

<u>Note from the Author, Timea Tokes:</u>

~o~

My dear, lovely Reader, thank you for taking the time to read my story! I really hope you enjoyed it as much as I did writing it. As always, your feedback is highly valued and much appreciated.

Please do take the time to scroll to the end of the book and leave a review. It would mean the World to me!

And remember, this story is all about your pleasure.

On the next page, you can learn a bit more about me and why I write, but you will also find author interviews (and much more) on my website.

~o~

ABOUT THE AUTHOR

~o~

I have been writing short stories and poems since a young age, but my ultimate goal was creating a novel. Or a series, rather. Now, with my four paranormal romance novels published, as well as more than 30 erotica titles under my belt, , I think I can say that it came true - but this only fuels my desire to write more. After all, we are allowed to dream the same dream (over and over again) - and that's exactly what I'm planning to do :)

I enjoy helping people in any way possible, and I really hope that my books will prove to be inspirational in a way. Whether readers are looking for a swift (and steamy) erotic story, or a paranormal romance, I want them to associate themselves with my characters and realize stuff about themselves in the process.

Yes, even the bad things. Because, in life, there is no black and white, only colors. Therefore, I don't think any of my characters are either good or bad, but rather a little bit of both.

Aren't we all?

Well, if you never had guilty thoughts, never had any self-confidence issues, or if you never wanted something (or someone) who belonged to someone else, then probably my books won't be for you. But, who knows, I might be able to show you a different perspective. I like to experiment with different genres, and new concepts and ideas.

I really enjoy learning as much as I can about people, what makes them tick (and live, laugh, cry, and sigh). In fact, I think our World (and those beyond) are so diverse, ten thousand lifetimes wouldn't be enough to explore it all. But one thing I truly believe in: those who belong in your life will find a way there. Therefore my stories are usually based on chance encounters and ordinary events that take an unexpected turn.

Like a blind date on Valentine's day, or a haircut, or a new job. Who says you can't meet someone 'accidentally'; while going to the hairdresser, someone you lost contact with 500 years ago? Trust me, you can. You just need to brace every day (and every book) with open eyes - and an open heart.

Just remember: my stories are all about you, and you alone. If they capture your attention (and your heart), then I've done my 'job'. I regularly try to release new content, both on Amazon and my blog. Please feel free to have a look, and sign up to my newsletter.

And, just so you know: I care about your opinion, very much so. Whether you liked my work or you didn't, I would be honored if you let me know what it meant for you. It would mean the world to me!

~o~

1. When did you create your first erotica story, and what was it about?

Well, my first story wasn't fully erotica, more a romance story. In fact, I never thought that one day I would write anything steamy. Not at all. I was shy, and grew up in an environment, where everything was taboo. Sharing my views on sex with anyone, let alone write about it? No way...

And yet, I soon had to realize that writing romantic stories couldn't happen without the couple getting it on eventually. Especially because the first four books series I created was about the same characters, and they are 100 pages each (which is a lot to go without including a sex scene every now and again). I must admit, I delayed the inevitable for as long as I could, just to realize later how much I enjoyed writing about sex.

Although my first attempts were very timid indeed, I tried to avoid being too explicit or descriptive. I concentrated on the romantic and paranormal aspect of it (the main characters dream about each other, and somehow when I was writing about the dreams, they gave me courage to be a bit braver).

But it wasn't until I started writing my erotic short stories in 2015, when I started to experiment. Well, if you have a look at 'The Good Neighbour', you can see how my explicitness and mood changed throughout the series.

I think I can say that this was the very first fully erotic story I created, fulfilling one of my secret fantasies (no, I don't have a hot neighbour, or at least I don't think I have, but the idea always fascinated me).

2. *What (or who) inspired you to start writing erotica?*

My own lack of courage, if I'm honest. All my friends were so open about their relationships and their fantasies, so I thought:

"Why do I have to be this way, when I want to explore everything that's out there?"

And as I have always enjoyed writing, I decided to try it out on paper. It started as a therapy I prescribed for myself, and then it escalated, taking me to places I never thought I would visit. I must say that I'm really glad I gave in to temptation.

3. *What do you find most challenging when writing these stories?*

To let them go when I finish writing them. I believe that it isn't possible, especially when I create a longer story. The characters, the feelings stay with me long after, as they become part of me for at least a little while.

Another aspect of it is that I keep thinking about what others read into them, and whether they convey their meaning in a way that I intended them to. But, just like when you give birth to a child, when writing a story as well you need to give it space after some time.

I once read a quotation (not sure where, or who said it, but it made me smile and I could definitely relate):

"I met the man of my dreams last night.. in chapter five..." *Sigh*

4. Do you write in other genres, and if yes, then would you consider mixing them with erotica?

Yes, and not sure. I ghost-write for a living, as well as create my own stories, which include romance, horror, thriller, fantasy, crime and more, but I'm not sure it would feel right to mix them with erotica. Mind that, I have had some strange requests that were a mixture, like fetish-horror, but it didn't actually include erotica. I suppose it could have, as it was about a foot fetish, which seems to be quite popular. Oh well, another thing to look at in the future :)

My favourite ones are psychological thrillers though, so I could probably turn one of those into erotica, but at the moment I'm thinking of a transition, rather than a mix. So, for example it would start as a thriller, but have a sexual ending. Hmm...

5. Have you written any stories that were inspired by real life events?

Yes. In fact, my very first story, 'Her First and Last Secret Admirer' (the four books I mentioned earlier) started with an actual recurring medieval dream, which I then implemented into the plot, creating a story and background for it. If it wasn't for that urge to put the whole thing into writing, I probably would never have picked up the courage to write at all. Now it is both in print and on Kindle, so I guess it was a nice bargain :)

I think that writing about real events, twisting them a little, but still keeping them close to your heart is an important process.

Also, that way you can relive those events over and over again, and others will keep guessing what was the real part in it.

Strangely enough, it adds to its mystery (and excitement, of course)...

6. What is your speciality and why?

I would say it's mixing the past with the present. I'm not an expert, but I also love to keep up the suspense until the end. Although this doesn't always come through in my erotic stories, as they are linear, but in my paranormal romance books, I draw a parallel between what happened 500 years ago and what's happening right now. It's difficult to explain without revealing the plot itself, but I do love to play with the mind of the reader, if you know what I mean.

7. Are there any topics you don`t like writing about?

Now? Not really. If you asked me a few years ago, I would have said everything that involves sex ;)

I guess I just realized that I shouldn't say no, just because I don't know how something feels. If I don't try it, I will never know... If I'm not familiar with a topic, then

I do my research, but not too many things scare me nowadays (without wanting to sound weird or vain).

8. Do you have any tips / warnings for newbie erotica writers?

Follow your dreams. You will get some ugly feedback (or none at all), but that doesn't mean that your work isn't appreciated. Don't take them personally, but accept them, so that they can serve as stepping stones, helping you improve your writing. We all make mistakes; that's what makes us human.

Personally, I couldn't wait to grab a physical copy of my books, and that made up for whatever negativity I got (but luckily it has only been minor stuff so far).

So, if you are thinking about writing, or if you already have a story or two, try to make them into a book, no matter how tiny it is. Trust me, as soon as you have it on your shelf, you will become a different person.

9. What is your favourite season and why?

Spring, because that's when everything comes to life. I just love to watch the flowers blossom and the world wake up from its winter slumber. I always feel like I'm reborn myself every time springs comes (I know, I'm a hopeless romantic).

www.ingramcontent.com/pod-product-compliance
Lightning Source LLC
Chambersburg PA
CBHW072141150726
48002CB00004B/1576